JIMMY CRACK CORN

by Candice F. Ransom
illustrations by Shelly O. Haas

Carolrhoda Books Inc., Minneapolis

For Marty—
a real trooper and a great friend–C.F.R.

To hope and the acknowledgment
in every young heart of its power–S.O.H.

Text copyright © 1994 by Candice F. Ransom
Illustrations copyright © 1994 by Shelly O. Haas

Carolrhoda Books Inc. ᶜ/o The Lerner Group
241 First Avenue North, Minneapolis, MN 55401

Library of Congress Cataloging-in-Publication Data
Ransom, Candice F.
   Jimmy Crack Corn / by Candice F. Ransom ; illustrated by
Shelly O. Haas.
      p.   cm.
   Summary: A nine-year-old boy and his father leave their
farm in Virginia to join other veterans marching on Washington,
D.C., to get the much-needed bonus money they had been
promised after World War I.
   ISBN 0-87614-786-4
   1. Bonus Expeditionary Force, 1932—Juvenile fiction.
[1. Bonus Expeditionary Force, 1932—Fiction. 2. Depressions—
1929—Fiction. 3. Washington (D.C.)—Fiction. 4. Fathers and
sons—Fiction.] I. Haas, Shelly O., ill. II. Title.
PZ7.R1743Ji   1994
[Fic]—dc20   93-16657
                                                 CIP
                                                  AC

Manufactured in the United States of America
1   2   3   4   5   6   P/JR   99   98   97   96   95   94

CONTENTS

Chapter One

The Last Chicken Sunday

Jimmy Watkins did not want to go into the barn. He knew what he would find there, and he did not want to see it.

"Jimmy," his father called, "I need your help."

Jimmy couldn't put it off anymore. He went into the barn.

Sunlight slanted through the open door, turning the black Model A a dusty yellow. Its wheels had been removed and now leaned against the wall. Jimmy thought their automobile looked crippled, like a bird with clipped wings. Cars were meant to *go* places, not to be propped up on wooden blocks in a barn. But they couldn't afford to buy gasoline for the car anymore.

"Help me with this battery," Jimmy's father said. Together they lifted the heavy battery out of the engine. Mr. Watkins set it on a shelf, next to the spark plugs he'd already removed.

"Now just a little oil in the cylinders," Mr. Watkins said, poking the oilcan into the engine. "That ought to keep it from rusting."

"Pa, how are you going to look for work now?" Jimmy asked.

"Shanks' mare."

"We don't have a horse," Jimmy said, puzzled. They didn't even have a cow anymore. His father had sold the cow last month to pay the taxes.

Jimmy's pa slammed the hood. "That's just a saying. 'Shanks' mare' means I'll walk."

Jimmy stared out the door at the road that went past their house. At one end was Washington, D.C. To the west, at the other end, were the Blue Ridge Mountains. Jimmy had never been to either place, but he knew the city was many miles away. It was an even longer distance to the mountains.

"Need me for anything else, Pa?" Jimmy asked. He hoped not. He wanted to finish his special project this afternoon.

"Nope. Thanks for your help." His father gave the car a final pat. "Have a nice rest, Betsy. We'll crank

you up again when these hard times are over." He turned his face into the shadows. Jimmy figured his pa hated to see the car up on blocks, too.

Outside, Jimmy reached into the branches of the chinaberry tree. From his secret hiding place, he took out the willow pipe he was whittling. He had once seen a picture of a fife carved out of wood. Jimmy hoped he could make music on his homemade pipe. Sitting in the shade of the tree, he began carving with his pocketknife.

Mr. Burke, their neighbor, had given Jimmy the knife last fall for picking up walnuts. It was a fine knife, but Jimmy wished Mr. Burke had paid him cash-money instead. He wanted to buy himself a trumpet. But cash-money was scarce these days. Jimmy knew that now more than ever, since his pa lost his job on the streetcar line.

Now Jimmy worried that he would have to sell his knife, the way Pa had to sell first the radio and then the cow. He thought about hiding the knife and saying he'd lost it.

Jimmy scooped out the core of the willow stick. Then he put it up to his eye. The hollow stick was like a telescope. Through the small circle, he saw a peculiar sight. A stranger was walking up their driveway. The man wore a battered felt hat and a patched coat, though it was a hot July day. Oddest of all were the man's pants. They were sewn from an oilcloth advertising hot dogs!

"Howdy, son," the hot dog man said. "Your ma or pa around?"

Jimmy's father came out of the barn. "Afternoon," he said to the stranger. "What can I do for you?"

The man swept off his hat. "Afternoon, sir. I was wondering if you had any odd jobs. See you got a big garden. I'm right handy with a hoe."

Jimmy's father shook his head. "Sorry. My son here hoes the garden."

Jimmy wished his father could hire the man. He

hated to hoe. "You're old enough to take over some of the chores," his father had said to Jimmy on his ninth birthday, a few weeks ago. Now Pa was always after him to pull weeds or haul water. If he had the money, Jimmy would hire the man to do those things for him.

The stranger seemed reluctant to give up. "If you have paper and a pencil, I'll draw a picture of your wife and children. All I ask is a bite to eat in return."

Mr. Watkins clapped the man on the back. "A traveling artist? Why didn't you say so? Come on in and meet the family. We'll be sitting down to the noon meal shortly. You're welcome to join us."

The stranger looked relieved. "Much obliged, sir. My name is John Stevens."

Jimmy followed his father and Mr. Stevens into the house. He knew why Pa was being so nice. The man was a hobo—one of the people without homes who tramped up and down the road day after day. Often they stopped at the Watkins place, asking for work or a handout. Jimmy's father wasn't the only man who had lost his job. But at least Jimmy's family still had a roof over their heads.

"Ma, we got company," Jimmy announced.

Mrs. Watkins turned from taking a pan of biscuits out of the oven. "How nice. We haven't had company for many a Sunday."

The smell of roast chicken cooling on the table made Jimmy's mouth water. Then he remembered this was their very last Chicken Sunday. Old Strawberry, the last hen from their flock, had been killed this morning.

Jimmy's mother killed and cooked a hen on the final Sunday of each month, as a treat. Sometimes the chicken was fried and sometimes it was roasted, but it was the only meat the Watkins family had until the next month. They couldn't afford to buy meat anymore.

They ate dried beans, biscuits, and flour gravy, even for breakfast. Jimmy liked biscuits and gravy, but he was getting pretty tired of beans. At least they'd have fresh vegetables when the garden started coming in.

"Mr. Stevens is an artist," Mr. Watkins said. "He's going to draw the children's pictures."

Jimmy's younger sister stared at the man. She had never seen a real artist before. Jimmy's little brother crawled out from under the kitchen table to tug on the stranger's homemade hot dog pants. "I'm four," he said, showing four sticky fingers.

Jimmy's mother laughed. "That's Carl Brooks and this is Rosemary. You've already met Jimmy. Dinner is ready."

As Jimmy sat down, he noticed that the stranger's eyes were glued to the chicken. He wondered if Mr. Stevens had eaten breakfast.

When the platter was passed to Jimmy, he reached for the biggest drumstick. Mr. Stevens's hungry eyes made him pause. It must have been a long time since the man had had a drumstick. Maybe he ought to let their guest have it.

Jimmy's stomach rumbled. This was their *last* Chicken Sunday. He took the drumstick, then passed the platter to Mr. Stevens. Mr. Stevens took a wing, the smallest part of the chicken.

"Don't you want the other drumstick?" Jimmy asked, surprised.

"I'm partial to wings," Mr. Stevens replied. "Let Carl Brooks have it. Growing boys just naturally need drumsticks."

Jimmy knew then that the man was just being polite. Mr. Stevens ate very fast, as if he hadn't had a real meal in days. Jimmy felt guilty gnawing on the chicken bone.

After dinner, Mrs. Watkins brought Mr. Stevens a crumpled sheet of brown wrapping paper, a stub of a pencil, and a board to use as a flat surface. "I hope this is all right," she apologized.

Mr. Stevens smoothed the paper over the board. "This will do just fine. Now, if you children will sit still for a few minutes. . . ."

His hand flew over the wrapping paper, sketching quickly. He held the board nearly flat as he worked.

Jimmy could see what he was drawing, though upside down. He watched as first Carl Brooks's babyish face, then Rosemary's thinner one, magically appeared under Mr. Stevens's flying pencil.

Mr. Stevens drew Jimmy last, a tall boy standing over his brother and sister. His dark hair, in need of cutting, fell across his broad forehead. In the picture, Jimmy's eyes were gazing off into the distance.

Then the artist scrawled his signature and the date in the bottom corner—"John Stevens, July 5, 1932."

Jimmy's ma and pa exclaimed over the picture.

"Such talent," said Mr. Watkins.

"Jimmy is talented, too," his mother told Mr. Stevens. "He sings like a meadowlark. Will you sing for us, Jimmy?"

"Yeah, Jimmy," Rosemary chimed in. "Sing your best song!"

Jimmy looked at the floor. He wasn't used to singing in front of strangers. He glanced up. Mr. Stevens gave him an encouraging smile. Jimmy did like the way Mr. Stevens had drawn his picture, as though Jimmy could see things Rosemary and Carl Brooks couldn't.

"Okay," he said. Rosemary and Carl Brooks always wanted him to sing his "best song," which was "Jimmy Crack Corn." They liked it so much, they even called him Jimmy Crack Corn.

Jimmy stood by the window and sang in a low voice:

Jimmy crack corn and I don't care,
Jimmy crack corn and I don't care,
Jimmy crack corn and I don't caare—

Mr. Stevens tapped his foot in time to the tune. "That boy should be on stage!"

Braver now, Jimmy launched into a new song he had heard on the radio, before his Pa had sold the radio

for cash-money. It was called "Life Is Just a Bowl of Cherries." Jimmy sang the verses good and loud, picturing a big bowl overflowing with juicy red cherries.

When Jimmy finished, Mr. Stevens stood up. "Thank you for dinner and the entertainment," he said, shaking Mr. Watkins's hand. "I'd best be on my way. It's a long hike to Washington."

"Looking for work?" Mr. Watkins asked.

"Me and eight million other fellas," the artist said with a laugh.

They waved good-bye from the doorway, watching Mr. Stevens's lanky figure trudge down the road toward Washington, D.C.

Mr. Watkins looked at Jimmy. "Did you hoe the lima beans?"

Jimmy frowned. "Not yet. Can I do it later?"

"Just so you get it done before dark." Jimmy's father went off to check the potato plants for bugs.

Jimmy sighed. Always it was work, work, work. In the old days, before hard times, they used to go for a drive on Sundays. But now that Betsy was up on blocks, they couldn't go anywhere.

He went outside to the chinaberry tree. At least he could finish his willow pipe before he had to hoe those dumb old lima beans. Rosemary and Carl Brooks tagged along after him.

"Sing 'Jimmy Crack Corn' again," Rosemary pleaded.

"Not now," Jimmy said. He didn't feel like singing.

Unlike the words of the song, Jimmy did care. He cared that today was the last Chicken Sunday. He cared that the car was up on blocks in the barn.

Life was not a bowl of cherries, Jimmy decided.

Chapter Two

Marching to Washington

From the daisy-dotted bank along the road, Jimmy watched his father set off down the highway. He was going to Alexandria, fifteen miles away, to look for odd jobs.

Jimmy worked in the garden until lunchtime. Rosemary brought Jimmy a jar of water and a biscuit to eat under the chinaberry tree. It was too hot to work in the afternoon, so Jimmy finished whittling his willow pipe.

He was disappointed with the pipe. When he put his fingers over the holes and blew, only a spitty sound came out—not the pure, clear musical note he'd hoped for. If only he had a real horn to make music.

It was nearly dark when Jimmy glimpsed his father dragging up the road. He ran out to meet him. "Did you get a job today, Pa?"

"Not today," Mr. Watkins sighed. "Maybe tomorrow."

But his father didn't find work the next day, either. Or the next. Jimmy could tell by his father's glum face when he plodded home that he hadn't found a job, so he quit asking.

They had biscuits and gravy every night for supper. Once, when Mrs. Watkins ran out of flour for gravy, they had biscuits and mustard. Jimmy thought it was good, but he wished he had something a little more filling. The next night, Mr. Watkins came home with a sack of flour.

Soon there were peas and young onions in the garden, and the string beans were "making," as Jimmy's mother said. Rosemary and Jimmy shelled peas on the porch. Rosemary wanted to eat the peas raw, but Jimmy wouldn't let her.

That night his mother fixed one of Jimmy's favorite dishes, creamed peas and onions. Jimmy ate until his stomach hurt.

After supper, Jimmy went outside. His father was hoeing the corn, slowly working the rows. He looked sad.

"What if you can't find a job?" Jimmy asked.

Mr. Watkins stopped hoeing to answer his son. "Oh,

we'll get along somehow. These aren't the first hard times I've seen in my life."

But these were the first hard times Jimmy had seen in *his* life, and he was worried. Every day, the number of men tramping up the highway grew larger. They were all looking for work. Looking for jobs that didn't seem to exist, no matter where they went or how far they walked.

Mr. Watkins saw the worried look on Jimmy's face. "We'll make out, Jimmy. One day we'll have a cow and a horse and chickens again."

"Will we be able to ride in Betsy again?"

"You bet. We may even get a new automobile, so Betsy won't get lonesome."

Two cars! Jimmy wondered how his father could dream such big dreams. "When are we going to have the horse and cow and the cars?" he wanted to know. And meat. When would they have meat on the table again?

"Soon," Mr. Watkins replied. "President Hoover keeps telling us that good times are just around the corner."

"What does that mean?"

His father leaned against the hoe. "It means we'll all have plenty of cash-money someday."

Jimmy tried to imagine what plenty of cash-money looked like. He pictured a room full of nickels.

Just then a truck rumbled to a halt at the bottom of their driveway. Men climbed out of the back and stepped out of the cab. The driver nodded at Jimmy's father. "Evening. Could we trouble you for some water?"

"Water we still have," Mr. Watkins joked. "Pump's over there."

The men lined up at the pump, drinking from the tin dipper. Some poured dipperfuls over their heads to rinse off road dust. "Where are you folks heading?" Mr. Watkins asked the driver.

"Washington, D.C."

Mr. Watkins shook his head. "You and everybody else. I hope you find work. I haven't been farther than Alexandria, myself, and I can tell you there isn't a job to be had in that town."

"Oh, we aren't looking for work," the driver informed him. "We're veterans, going to Washington to get the bonus Congress promised us."

"I heard about you fellas," Mr. Watkins said. "Read about you in the paper. Call yourselves bonus marchers?"

"Some of us are riding," the driver joked. "But we're after the same thing, no matter how we get there. Our bonus."

"Think you'll get it?" Mr. Watkins asked.

"We're sure going to try," said the driver. "The U.S.

government said it would pay the money in '45. We need it now. After all, we served our country. Now it's time our country served us."

The men filed back into the truck, some with dripping hair. The driver tipped his hat at Jimmy and his father. "Much obliged," he said, getting behind the wheel of the truck.

"Good luck!" Mr. Watkins called over the roar of the engine.

"Good luck!" Jimmy added, waving as the truck backfired down the road. Then he asked, "What was that man talking about, Pa? Who'd they say they were?"

"Veterans," his father explained. "They fought in the

Great War in Europe. They plan to camp out in Washington until Congress gives them the bonus money it owes them."

Jimmy was still confused. "Why should the government give veterans money?"

"We got paid while we were fighting, but after the war Congress decided we should get extra money, a bonus.

Jimmy realized his father had said "we." "Did you fight in that war, Pa?"

"Yes, I did. I was a doughboy in France."

"A what?"

His father smiled. "Doughboy. That's what American infantrymen were called over there. Because of our helmets, I guess. They were kind of doughnut shaped."

Jimmy was surprised. His father had fought in the Great War and he never knew it until this very second. "You never told me," he said. "When were you there, Pa?"

His father sounded tired. "A long time ago, Jimmy. The war lasted from 1914 to 1918. America didn't get into it until 1917. But we did our part." His father picked up his hoe and began hacking at weeds again.

Jimmy had always thought his father was a strong man, but now he noticed that his father's shoulders were bowed. His pa worked hard. The men that were going to Washington looked worn-out, too. It would be a happy day when the president handed those men the bonus money on the steps of the Capitol.

Suddenly Jimmy had an idea. Why shouldn't his pa get *his* bonus from the president? After all, he had fought in the war, too. His pa deserved the bonus every bit as much as those other men. "Pa," he cried. "You ought to march to Washington, too. Get *your* money!"

His father straightened up. "March to Washington?" he repeated. "What foolishness, Jimmy. Who would take care of the place here?"

"I would," Jimmy offered with a gulp. He didn't really like to work. But his father *had* said he was old enough to help out. "I can take care of Ma and Rosemary and Carl Brooks."

"I don't believe those marchers are going to force Congress to give them the money," his father said.

"But you don't know," Jimmy insisted. "You have to try."

His father looked at him, considering. "It isn't that far from here . . . maybe I should try." He shouldered the hoe. "Let's talk this over with your mother. See what she says."

Mrs. Watkins listened to the story of the bonus marchers. When Jimmy and his father finished talking, she said simply, "Well, you must go. Take Jimmy with you. He'll keep you company. And it'll do the boy a world of good to get out of here for a few days."

Jimmy's heart leaped. March to Washington with his father! He wouldn't have to work in the garden. He'd get to see the Washington Monument and the White House and the Capitol. . . .

"Nora, it might be more than a few days," Mr. Watkins said.

"I'll be fine. There isn't that much to do around here since we got rid of the cow and the chickens. Mr. Burke will look in on us."

Mr. Watkins smiled at Jimmy. "Looks like you and me are going to march to Washington. We'll leave at first light tomorrow."

Jimmy was too excited to get much sleep. He sat up in the bed he shared with Carl Brooks, wondering if daybreak would ever come. When the first pale ribbons of light streaked the sky, he bounded out of bed and grabbed the bundle of clothes he'd packed the night before.

His brother and sister were still asleep, but by the time he got dressed, his mother was up and his father was ready to leave.

Jimmy's mother handed him a sack of biscuits and a mason jar of water. "Be careful," she said and kissed them both good-bye.

"Don't worry, Ma," Jimmy said. "We'll come back

with that bonus money and our troubles will be over. I'll even bring you a present."

Jimmy and his father walked down the road toward Washington. The air smelled clean with promise. Jimmy was sure the president would be waiting with their bonus money as soon as they marched into Washington.

He stared at a house with a sagging front porch and a rusted iron pot in the yard. He had seen the house before but didn't know who lived there. These people were probably having hard times, too.

After an hour of walking, they stopped to have breakfast. One biscuit each, washed down with water.

"Are we almost there?" Jimmy asked his father. His boots were rubbing blisters on his heels. He wished he had a new pair, but new boots cost a lot of money. If he did have any money, he'd buy a trumpet, not boots.

"If we make it by sundown, we'll be doing good," Mr. Watkins replied.

Sundown! Jimmy knew the city was far away, but he never realized it was that far away.

A truck packed with men pulled over. "Need a lift?" the driver shouted out the window. More bonus marchers! The men in the back made room for Jimmy and his father.

"We're marching, too," Jimmy said proudly. "We're going to get our bonus money."

A man who had no front teeth laughed. "The more the merrier. Won't Hoover love this tea party?"

The truck putt-putted down the road, eating up miles that would have taken Jimmy and his father forever to walk. Jimmy clung to the rail around the bed of the truck, marveling at the countryside unraveling behind him. After a while the driver shouted, "Potomac ahead!"

Jimmy stood up to glimpse the famous river. It was as wide as the ocean, with rocks and little islands scattered around. The truck scudded across the bridge, and then they were in Washington, D.C.

Chapter Three

The Hobo Camp

The truck stopped just on the other side of the bridge. It was early afternoon, and the sun was high and hot. The men tumbled out. Some began strapping home-made signs to their backs. One sign read, "Remember 1917–1918."

Jimmy was silent as he joined the men walking down the street. He fell two paces behind his father as he gawked at the tall buildings. And the sidewalk! He'd never seen concrete sidewalks before. His father used to work in Alexandria, where there were trolleys and sidewalks, but Jimmy had never been there. He longed to skip down the sidewalk, but they were marching right down the middle of the road. Cars and buses had

to wait for them to pass.

"Are we going to the White House now to get our money?" Jimmy wanted to know. President Hoover should be waiting for them, with crisp new bills for each of the bonus marchers.

His father shook his head. "According to these fellas, we're going to a camp they've set up. A lot of veterans are here already. We all have to stick together."

A camp! That sounded exciting to Jimmy. Maybe he would see more hoboes. They led adventurous lives, free as birds, riding the rails in empty boxcars from city to city. Every railroad yard had a hobo jungle—a camp for hoboes. There they cooked food in a big stew pot and told stories around the fire.

Jimmy marched past towering government buildings, past parks with statues. In the distance, he saw the white dome of the Capitol and the stately Washington Monument. After a while, they crossed another bridge, under which the oil-slicked Anacostia River flowed.

On the other side was an amazing sight. An entire village fashioned from cardboard, tin, and other pieces of scrap sprawled along the muddy flats. One of the men grinned at Jimmy. "Welcome to Camp Marks."

"Looks like a Hooverville to me," another man commented.

Jimmy had heard about the homemade towns people built when they lost their homes. "Hoovervilles" were named after the president. Many blamed President Hoover for the hard times. Jimmy thought this place looked like the biggest hobo camp in the world. Mr. Watkins laughed at Jimmy's awestruck face. "We have to build ourselves a place to stay. Are you game?"

Jimmy was game. Winding their way through the "streets," they came to a huge dump. Men picked through the trash, hunting for building materials and other things they could use. Jimmy found a sheet of corrugated iron that was too heavy for him to lift. He put his foot on it to claim ownership until his father could haul it away. Mr. Watkins scrounged a section of stovepipe and some peeling plywood.

They spent the rest of the afternoon building their makeshift house. Jimmy's father constructed a three-sided lean-to with the plywood. The iron sheet became the roof. An old blanket served as a doorway.

Jimmy furnished their new house with more treasures from the junk pile. An egg crate became a table. An automobile fender turned upside down and lined with a saggy cushion made a good chair.

After their house was finished, Jimmy asked his father if he could go exploring.

"Don't get lost," Mr. Watkins warned.

"I won't," Jimmy promised, racing off.

Camp Marks was better than a carnival. The huts weren't very colorful and the smells from the riverfront made Jimmy's nose wrinkle, but there was something interesting going on everywhere he looked.

A man pounded nails straight with a rock. A group of men in their BVD underwear tops sat around a gramophone, listening to a scratchy-sounding record. Jimmy hung around the gramophone a while. He'd always wanted one. Anything that made music fascinated him.

Farther down the flats, a woman cleaned the inside of a rusty old automobile. Children played in the dust. Jimmy realized with amazement that the family lived in the car.

He stopped at a shack where a man played a harmonica. "Is it hard to play one of those?" he asked the man.

"Not at all. Want to try?" The man pulled up the orange crate next to him. He was a lot older than Jimmy's father. Eagerly Jimmy sat down and took the harmonica.

"What's your name, son?" asked the man.

"Jimmy Watkins."

"Short for James?" the man asked. Jimmy nodded. "Then you should go by James. Never been partial to nicknames."

"James is my father's name, too. Everybody calls me Jimmy. My sister calls me Jimmy Crack Corn. What's your name?"

"Foster Morris."

"Foster Morris," Jimmy repeated wonderingly. "With a name that grand, you must be somebody important."

Mr. Morris laughed. He wore patched blue trousers held up with rope suspenders. His shirt had so many holes in it, Jimmy didn't know how it stayed on his back. His clothes might have seen better days, but Mr. Morris's laugh was rich and hearty.

"Oh, me!" he gasped when he could speak. "I'm important, all right. Haven't had a job in two years—I expect I'll dine with Hoover tonight."

"Really?" Jimmy was impressed.

WAR SONGS

TENTING ON THE OLE CAMP TOWN

"Just kidding. Now, blow easy into the harmonica.
You'll get the hang of how to make notes."

The harmonica was harder to play than Jimmy had
thought. But he practiced doggedly until he could play
"Twinkle, Twinkle, Little Star." At last he was making music!

Suddenly he realized it was getting late. "My pa will
be worried about me," he said, handing Mr. Morris his
harmonica. "I've got to get back."

Mr. Morris pushed the harmonica into Jimmy's pocket. "Keep it, James. You play better than I do."

Jimmy was dumbfounded. No one had ever given

him such a magnificent gift for nothing. What a day! First he'd marched into Washington, then he and his father had built a fine house, and now he had a harmonica.

"Gee, thanks, Mr. Morris. When I'm a famous trumpet player, I'll tell everybody Mr. Foster Morris gave me a harmonica."

Mr. Morris laughed his deep, rich laugh. "You do that, James."

Jimmy liked Mr. Morris a lot. He was sure his father would, too. "Come eat supper with us," he said.

"I could use the company." Mr. Morris lumbered to his feet. "And I'll show your pa how to get provisions around here. It isn't easy."

As they walked, Mr. Morris told Jimmy he had been at Camp Marks since the end of June. He'd come all the way from New York City to collect his bonus.

At the foot of the bluff, overlooking the river, a pig rooted inside a small pen. "That's the camp mascot," Mr. Morris said. "His name is Andy Mellon."

"Even the pigs have fancy names here," Jimmy remarked.

Mr. Morris smiled. "Andrew Mellon is President Hoover's secretary of treasury. He's got more money than he knows what to do with. Naturally, he's dead-set against paying the veterans their bonus."

Jimmy was even more interested in the small crowd bent over a pipe sticking out of the ground. "What is that?"

"Some fool had himself buried in a wooden box underground," Mr. Morris replied with a disdainful shake of his head. "He breathes through that pipe and is fed soup down it."

"Why did he bury himself?" Was there no end to the marvels of Camp Marks?

"It's a gimmick," Mr. Morris said. "You can look at him through that tube—for a penny."

Now Jimmy's attention was fastened on two men dancing a jig on a platform set up near the center of camp.

"People give speeches up there," Mr. Morris explained. "But when nobody's giving a speech, the stage is free to anyone who wants to perform. Why don't you go on up and play a tune on the harmonica?" The man's eyes sparkled with amusement.

"Not me," Jimmy said. But then he saw the pennies people threw on the stage. The dancers quickly scooped up the change while the audience laughed good-naturedly. "Would they throw money at me?" he asked Mr. Morris.

"Only if you're good. No telling what they'd throw if you're bad."

Jimmy didn't think about that part. He saw a way to

earn money for the trumpet he wanted. He clambered up onto the stage. But once he was up there, he was frozen with fright. His feet finally came unglued, and he started to slide off the stage.

"Hey, boy, what are you going to do?" a man in an army hat yelled at him.

Jimmy swallowed. He couldn't slink away now.

"Tell us what you're going to do!" another voice called.

"I'm going to sing," Jimmy said.

"Well," cackled an old man, "go to it!"

Jimmy got to it. He began with "Life Is Just a Bowl of Cherries." The audience clapped and whistled. Then he sang his family's favorite, "Jimmy Crack Corn." The audience liked his singing so much, he sang every song he knew.

"That's all," Jimmy said, turning to leave the stage. They weren't going to throw money at him! Maybe they didn't like him after all.

Suddenly the crowd began tossing pennies at his feet. Jimmy gathered the coins in his hat and leaped off the stage. He must have collected twenty cents—maybe more! Making money this way was easy. He'd never have to hoe the garden again.

"They gave me cash-money!" Jimmy cried to his new friend.

"You deserved it," Mr. Morris said. "You have a fine singing voice, James Watkins."

Jimmy half-ran, half-skipped to his father's hut. Mr. Watkins was stirring a pot that hung over a small fire. "There you are," he said when he saw Jimmy. "I was just about to go hunting for you."

"Pa, look what I got! Just for singing!" Jimmy turned his cap upside down on the egg-crate table. Pennies spilled out, glistening in the firelight.

Mr. Watkins grinned at Jimmy. "Seems to me like you got *your* bonus."

Chapter Four

The
Answer
at Last

"This is Mr. Morris," Jimmy said breathlessly. "Can he eat supper with us?"

"Of course," Jimmy's father replied. "Don't know how it tastes, but there's plenty of it."

When Mr. Morris saw what Jimmy's father was stirring in the pot, he shook his head. "We can do better than this. Be right back." He disappeared into the camp, leaving Jimmy and his father to watch the simmering pot.

"Mr. Morris is real nice," Jimmy said. "Look what he gave me." He fished his harmonica from his pocket and played a few bars.

"You made out better today than I did," Mr. Watkins

said with a laugh. "The only thing I could find to eat was a few old potatoes. I guess Mr. Morris doesn't like potato mush."

Jimmy told his father about the exciting sights he had seen around the camp. "I was going to use one of my pennies to talk to that man buried underground," he said.

"Well, you earned it," his father said agreeably.

"But I don't know if it's worth it," Jimmy continued thoughtfully. "Mr. Morris said it was a gimmick."

Mr. Watkins patted Jimmy on the shoulder. "Now you're learning the value of a penny. Your mother was right. It has done you good to see new places."

Jimmy didn't admit he was saving his pennies to buy himself a trumpet.

Mr. Morris returned. He carried a bunch of wild onions in one hand and a sliver of fatty bacon wrapped in newspaper in the other.

"Fix that mush right up," he said. He got busy mincing the onions with his pocketknife. He fried the bacon crisp in a pot lid that served as a frying pan, then added the onions and bacon to the potato mush. From one of his pockets he produced a tin of salt.

"Always carry it," he proclaimed. He sprinkled a little salt in the pot.

They sat cross-legged on the ground to eat from the

pot. Jimmy's spoon was really a flat piece of metal his father had curved to make a slight bowl. The mush was delicious.

"You're a fine cook," Mr. Watkins said to the older man.

"Ought to be," Mr. Morris replied. "I was head chef at a big hotel in Manhattan."

"New York City?" said Mr. Watkins admiringly.

"I knew you were somebody important," Jimmy crowed.

Mr. Morris laughed. Then he left again, this time to bring a small chest to their hut. Inside the chest were several objects. A U.S. flag and a string-tied bundle of thick cards were on top.

"Where did you get the flag?" Jimmy asked.

"In France," replied Mr. Morris. "Like most of the fellas here, I was in the Great War."

He untied the bundle and handed Jimmy one of the cards. Jimmy tried to read it, but the gold lettering was too fancy.

"These are menus," Mr. Morris explained. "People would come to eat in the restaurant of my hotel, even if they were staying in another hotel."

Jimmy touched the faded cards. Mr. Morris sounded sad as he talked about his days as a chef. He seemed lonely. Jimmy wondered if Mr. Morris would want to stay with them. "Pa's a terrible cook," he said, hoping his father's feelings wouldn't be hurt. "Will you be our—what did you call it—our chef?"

Again the rich laugh boomed. Mr. Morris ruffled Jimmy's hair. "I'd be delighted, James. But only if you peel the potatoes. Head chefs do not peel potatoes."

Life at Camp Marks was not much different from life at home, Jimmy observed after they had been in Washington a week. Food was the most important subject, just like at home.

Jimmy quickly learned there weren't many provisions to feed the thousands of veterans camped on the Anacostia Flats. They had something called mulligan stew almost every day. "Water and anything that can be boiled in it," was Mr. Morris's description. Sometimes they had beans and bread, but mostly stew.

Water for showers was scarce, too. Jimmy stood in line every morning to duck his head under a hose connected to a fire hydrant.

Yet the men stayed. A sign on one shack read, "We're Not Budging!" Jimmy gulped when he read the sign on another hut: "Stay Till 1945." He hoped they wouldn't have to stay *that* long to get their bonus. But it began to seem that way.

At first Jimmy kept busy exploring the camp, but then the routine began to be tiresome. Camp life wasn't as exciting as it had been when Jimmy and his father first arrived. The man buried in the box underground was dug up by the police. Jimmy learned that the man's partner, the one who collected the pennies, had run off with the money. On sunny days, the men played ball. Sometimes a wrestling match was held in the center of camp. But mostly people played cards and sat around. He wondered what Rosemary and Carl Brooks were doing at home. He wondered if his mother was able to do all the chores.

Every day Jimmy's father walked across the Anacostia River with some other veterans to wait on the steps of the capitol building. Every day Jimmy thought his father would say the president had finally handed over their bonus.

Mr. Watkins spent each day talking to men from different parts of the country. "Hard times are everywhere," he reported to Jimmy one evening. "Wouldn't pay us to move to a new state—we'd have the same troubles. Maybe worse troubles."

The days dragged by. Jimmy sang on the stage almost every night. He stored his earnings in an empty tobacco sack.

One hot day, after nearly two weeks at Camp Marks, Jimmy went to the riverside, beneath the bluffs, to practice his harmonica.

"So you're the music boy," said a voice above him.

Jimmy looked up to see a boy and a girl, both with carrot-orange hair. The boy was about his age. He guessed they were brother and sister. The boy scrambled down the bluff to join Jimmy. The girl slipped and slid down behind him.

"Who calls me the music boy?" Jimmy wanted to know.

"Everybody. You're famous. I bet you've made a hundred dollars singing," answered the girl. She seemed younger than her brother, maybe seven or eight. Both of them were scarecrow-skinny.

"Nah. More like three dollars." Jimmy counted his

pennies every night before he went to sleep. He liked singing so much, he still couldn't believe people actually paid him to do it. "I'm going to buy a trumpet. And a present for my mother. 'Cept I don't know what to get her."

"How about a Flossie Flirt doll?" the girl suggested.

Her brother laughed. "That's what *you* want."

"So?" The girl's face turned as fiery-colored as her hair. "Want to make something of it?"

"I don't think my mother would want a doll," Jimmy said quickly to prevent a fight. "My sister would, though. But I don't have enough to buy Rosemary a doll and a present for my mother *and* a trumpet."

"Seems like a lot of money to me," the girl said, nudging a pebble with her bare foot. "We've never even seen three whole dollars, not all at once."

"We have, too!" her brother argued.

"Have not!"

"Look," Jimmy interrupted, "why don't you come back to our place and I'll show it to you. My name is Jimmy Watkins. I'm here with my pa."

"I'm Patrick O'Brian," the boy said. "And this is my bratty sister Kathy." Kathy stuck out her tongue at her brother.

Jimmy led the way back to camp. "How come I haven't seen you two before?"

"We just got here yesterday," Patrick replied. "We should have been here a month ago, but our car kept breaking down."

"And then Eddie—he's the baby—got sick and we had to wait till he got better," Kathy put in. Jimmy noticed that Patrick and Kathy liked to take turns talking. They were probably very close, even if they did fight a lot.

"There's six of us," Patrick said to Jimmy. "Eight, if you count my ma and pa. We thought there'd be a place to stay when we got here. We had to sleep in the car last night. We've been sleeping in the car so long, I can't remember what it's like to sleep in a bed anymore."

"I have to sleep with my head under the steering wheel," Kathy said. "One night I sat up too fast and got a big knot on my head."

Patrick made a face. "At least you get the seat. Try sleeping on the floorboard."

Jimmy realized how lucky he and his father were to have a hut of their own. It wasn't the best place in the world, but at least they weren't piled in a car.

Mr. Morris was cooking supper outside the Watkinses' hut. "Couldn't even rustle up potatoes today," he said ruefully. "I'm afraid it's onion soup or nothing, James."

Jimmy still had trouble getting used to being called

"James." No one called him that at home.

"That's okay," said Jimmy. "You make good onion soup." To his new friends he said, "This is Mr. Foster Morris. He used to be a chef in a New York hotel. That means he was an important cook."

"Now I'm camp cook," Mr. Morris joked. "And who might you two be?"

Jimmy introduced Patrick and Kathy. "They just got here yesterday," he told Mr. Morris. "They have eight people in their family, and they're sleeping in their car!"

"Is that right?" Mr. Morris noticed that Patrick and Kathy seemed very interested in the soup. "Would you like to sample my soup? Let me know if I've got too much salt in it." He dished up three cans of the pungent-smelling broth.

Jimmy had never seen anybody eat as fast as Patrick. The can was emptied in a flash. Mr. Morris refilled it. "Have some more. It's hard to give an opinion on just one taste."

Patrick drank his can of broth a little slower this time. He handed the empty can back to Mr. Morris. "That was real good. I think you have just the right amount of salt. We're going to have a big supper tonight—my pa promised. Roast turkey, maybe."

Jimmy wondered where the O'Brians were getting a turkey to roast. Food grew scarcer with each passing

day. He started to ask Patrick about this, but Mr. Morris shook his head.

"And a seven-layer cake," Kathy chimed in. "With gobs and gobs of pink frosting."

"Of course you are," Mr. Morris agreed. "We'll all eat like lords and ladies when we get our bonus, won't we?"

Suddenly Jimmy understood why Patrick and Kathy kept talking about the fancy food they were going to have. It was make-believe, like the two cars his father dreamed of having one day. Talking about food helped them live with their hunger.

"You can buy that Flossie Flirt doll," Jimmy said. "And I'll get my trumpet. Hey, here's my pa."

Mr. Watkins trudged through the camp. He had spent the day as usual, on the steps of the Capitol, waiting for an answer about the bonus.

"Did you hear?" Jimmy asked eagerly. Maybe today was the day they'd have good news. His father didn't look very happy, but he was probably tired from the heat.

"Yes, I heard," his father said, sitting down wearily. "Congress voted down the bill. They will not pay us our bonus early. The answer is no."

Chapter Five

The Hardest
Time of All

Mr. Watkins's words dropped into a stunned silence, like stones in an empty bucket. Patrick cleared his throat. "Well, me and Kathy better be moving along," he said, and they left.

"Pa, is it true? We aren't getting any money at all?" Jimmy whispered. He couldn't believe they had come all this way, and stayed all this time, for nothing.

"It's true, all right." Mr. Watkins wiped his forehead with the back of his hand. Heat lay over the camp like a wool blanket.

"Well, that's it, then," Foster Morris said glumly. "It's over for all of us."

He rummaged around in the small chest he used to

store his belongings. He pulled out the pasteboard menus he had once proudly shown Jimmy and Mr. Watkins.

"These bits of paper are all I have left," he said. "I'm too old for cooking—too old even to be a dishwasher. I have no friends, no place to go, no money, and no prospects."

Jimmy had thought his father's words were the saddest he'd ever heard, but Mr. Morris's confession made his chest tighten. Mr. Morris shuffled off, still clutching his menus.

"Mr. Morris, where are you going?" Jimmy called. He started after his friend.

Jimmy's father gently pulled him back. "Leave him be, Jimmy."

"But what's he going to do, Pa?" Jimmy demanded. "He hasn't got a home or any family. What's going to happen to him?"

His father sighed. "That's a question a lot of people will be asking themselves tonight."

It was quiet in the camp that evening. No one climbed up on the stage to dance or tell jokes or give a speech. Jimmy did not feel like singing. He didn't even feel like playing his harmonica. He just sat on his pallet inside the hut until it was time to go to sleep.

The next morning, it was business as usual in the

camp. People stood in line to fill washtubs or take a shower. Others stood in line for food. They mended clothes, played cards, and swapped stories. But they didn't leave. Jimmy was surprised. He thought everyone would be packing to go home.

"Why are they staying?" he asked his father as they ate cold beans for breakfast.

"They don't have anyplace else to go," Mr. Watkins replied. "We have a home, at least. And we have each other to share the hard times."

A desolate air hung over the camp. Jimmy wished the camp was like it had been in the beginning, when it was new and exciting. Sleeping on a pallet was fun at first, but now he longed for his own bed. He missed eating at a table, off a real plate with a real fork. Their supper might be only beans and cornbread, but Jimmy's mother always had flowers in a jam jar on the table.

"Living rough," as the hoboes called it, wasn't as great as Jimmy had thought it would be. He had believed life on the road was an endless adventure. But never knowing where your next meal was coming from wasn't much fun after a while.

"I miss Ma," Jimmy told his father. "And Rosemary and Carl Brooks. I even miss the garden."

"It's time we went home," his father agreed, getting to his feet. "I'll see what I can do."

When Mr. Watkins returned a short time later, Jimmy looked up hopefully. "Are we going home?" he asked.

"Yes, but not right away," his father answered. "A bunch of fellas are sharing a ride. They'll take us home, but they need some time to get organized." He ruffled Jimmy's hair. "Think you can stay here a little longer?"

"Yeah. I can play with Patrick and Kathy." Even though Jimmy wanted to go home, he knew he would miss his new friends.

In the days that followed, Jimmy and Patrick and Kathy played along the riverfront. They fished and searched for smooth, white pebbles and talked away the long, hot afternoons. Jimmy missed Mr. Morris. He guessed the man had left the camp.

The day before Jimmy and his father planned to go home, Jimmy walked over to the O'Brian campsite. The whole family was still living in their car. Patrick ran over to greet Jimmy.

"Guess what!" he said. "We're going to California!"

"California!" Jimmy said with wonder. "That's clear across the country!"

"Three thousand miles." Patrick was so excited, his red hair stood on end. "We're going to Hollywood. Movie stars! Won't that be great? My dad says we can pick oranges and make a fortune. If we get hungry, we can just pick our supper." He grinned at Jimmy. "Why don't you and your pa come along with us?"

Jimmy shook his head. "We can't go to California. We have to go home. Ma's waiting for us."

"Well, I'll send you a postcard of the Pacific Ocean."

"I'd like that," Jimmy said. "When are you leaving?"

"This morning. Soon as my pa rounds up some gasoline."

Jimmy stared at the car. It didn't look as though it would make a long journey. The tires were worn and one window was broken. He remembered from his geography book that there were mountains and a scorching desert to cross. But the O'Brians were going to California anyway. Hard times could not beat that family.

Jimmy was sorry to see them go. Patrick and Kathy were his closest friends at the camp, next to Mr. Morris. If only he had something to give them. A going-away present.

"Wait here," he told Patrick. "Don't leave before I get back."

Jimmy raced back through the camp to his hut. Kneeling on his pallet, he fished the tobacco sack from under his makeshift mattress. He held the sack in his

hand. His trumpet money. When would he ever hold that much money again? Still, Patrick and his family needed it more. Jimmy dashed back to the O'Brian campsite.

Mr. O'Brian was pouring gasoline from a can into the car. Patrick was helping Kathy round up the little kids.

"Here," Jimmy said. He pressed the sack into Patrick's hand.

Patrick emptied the sack into his palm. He looked up at Jimmy with astonishment. "This is your singing money. You were saving it to buy a trumpet."

"I know," Jimmy said. "But I want you and Kathy to have it instead."

"I'll send you the biggest box of oranges I can find," Patrick promised. "Straight from California."

They laughed and then it was time to say good-bye. Jimmy waved at the car until Patrick and Kathy's red heads were specks in the distance.

Jimmy felt sad. All his friends were leaving. First Mr. Foster Morris, and now Patrick and Kathy. More than ever, he wanted to go home.

Suddenly a commotion broke out in the camp. People were darting in and out of tents and huts, calling to each other in loud, urgent voices. What was going on?

A man accidentally pushed Jimmy. Jimmy fell, skinning his shin. Another man picked him up. "Son, if I was you, I'd skedaddle. The troops are coming."

"What troops?" gasped Jimmy.

"The U.S. government, that's who. The very same army I risked my neck for in France. Now they're coming to clear us out." Seeing that Jimmy was all right, the man rushed off.

The army was coming! He'd better find his father. Jimmy dashed through the mob, dodging mothers hunting for lost children, and men with bedsprings on their backs. A man tripped over the boxes he was carrying. "Go on without me!" he yelled hoarsely to his wife and children.

Something exploded in front of Jimmy, emitting a noxious gas. His nose and eyes burned. Tears streaming from his eyes, he staggered up a hill, away from the tear gas fumes.

A spark of orange caught Jimmy's eye. The soldiers were using torches to set the huts on fire. Some veterans angrily lit torches of their own from the blaze and ignited the makeshift houses. Babies bawled and the wail of ambulances could be heard across the river, heading toward the camp. Jimmy raced through the churning crowd to the hut he shared with his father. "Pa!" he screamed over the racket.

There was no answer.

He threw himself inside. Their lean-to was empty.

His father was gone. Choked with fright, Jimmy grabbed a man who was struggling with a crate of canned goods. "Mister," he croaked. "Have you seen my pa? His name is James Watkins, same as mine, and he—"

"Sorry, boy, I haven't time. The Twelfth Infantry is on our heels!" He jerked away, staggering into the crowd.

Jimmy stood like a wooden cigar-store Indian as hundreds of people tore past him. Flames licked all sides of the camp. Smoke stung his eyes. He reeled as someone knocked him down again. This time no one helped him up.

Through blurred eyes, he saw the troops—soldiers on horseback with swords and bayonets. They pushed the mob along in front of them like a street sweeper with a broom. Horrified, Jimmy watched as a woman fell under the flailing hooves of a horse. The soldiers were coming his way!

Where was his father? How would he ever find him in this mob? Suppose he was hurt? Suppose he was trapped in a burning hut?

A man snatched roughly at his shirt. Jimmy fought him off. "Leave me alone!" he screeched. "I have to find my pa!"

"James, it's me!" a voice bellowed.

He looked up into Foster Morris's face. His knees felt rubbery with relief. "Mr. Morris! I thought you'd left. Where have you—?"

"No time to chitchat," Mr. Morris said, pulling Jimmy out of the way. "Now hurry, or we'll get run over."

Together they lurched along with the throng of men, women, and children fleeing the soldiers. The soldiers threw canisters of tear gas and set fire to the few huts not already in flames.

Jimmy had never been so frightened. The soldiers on horseback jabbed their bayonets at the men who tried to hold their ground. He saw one man struck on the side of the head. The man dropped to his knees, his scalp bleeding. People nearly trampled him.

If only there was some way to stop the panic, Jimmy thought. He remembered his harmonica. It was still in his pocket! Putting the harmonica to his lips, he began to play "Jimmy Crack Corn." The bright, familiar tune cut through the screams and yells. People still ran wildly, but those nearby began to slow down.

"This way!" Mr. Morris yelled, waving his hand. "Follow us!"

People saw his upraised hand and scrambled up the hill after them. Jimmy kept on playing. Like the Pied Piper in the fairy story, Jimmy led people out of the camp.

As they retreated into the woods, Jimmy noticed that
Mr. Morris carried his faded flag and his precious
menus tucked under one arm. Jimmy hadn't had time
to save anything from their camp. He was glad he had
given his singing money to the O'Brians.

He stopped playing the harmonica to catch his
breath. Beside him, Mr. Morris gasped for air. Jimmy
realized Mr. Morris was an old man. Running up the
bluff had been too much for him.

Then Jimmy saw a sight that turned his blood to ice.
"Mr. Morris!" he shrieked. "Look out!"

A soldier was galloping right at them, his bayonet
flashing in the firelight.

Chapter Six

James,
Sometimes

The horse bore down on them, its iron-shod hooves
kicking up tufts of grass. Jimmy thought the soldier
was going to run right over them, but at the last possi-
ble second, he yanked the horse's reins. The animal
veered sharply, missing Jimmy and Mr. Morris by a hair.

"Move along, there," the soldier barked.

Jimmy was ready to flee, but Mr. Morris was still
panting for air. "Can't you see he can't catch his
breath?" Jimmy cried to the soldier.

"My orders are to clear you people out of the city,"
the soldier said. "Keep moving." Then he spied the
faded flag under Mr. Morris's arm.

"Where did you get that flag?" he demanded, leaning

forward from the saddle. With the tip of his bayonet, he reached for the flag.

Now Jimmy was angry. He had been taught to respect the army, but this was too much. Driving old men and women and children till they were ready to drop—it just wasn't fair. And now they were trying to take Mr. Morris's flag! Poor Mr. Morris was gasping like a hooked bass, unable to defend himself.

Thrusting himself in front of his friend, Jimmy looked defiantly at the soldier. He was still afraid of the deadly bayonet pointed at his chest, but he was madder than he was scared.

"Leave him alone!" he exclaimed. "That's his flag, not yours! He had that flag in France—"

"And he'll fight for it here, if he has to," a voice broke in. A shabby figure approached them. The man's face was smoke stained, but Jimmy knew those bright eyes at once.

"Pa!" Forgetting the soldier, Jimmy flung himself at his father. He was never so glad to see anyone in his life. "How did you find us?"

"I heard the harmonica," his father said.

"Pa, they're making us leave!"

"Yes, they are," Mr. Watkins said, meeting the soldier's gaze without fear. "One day you will be a veteran yourself," he said to the soldier. "And you'll

understand what this rally was all about."

"And you'll be ashamed you took part in it," Mr. Morris wheezed.

"I didn't want to come, anyhow," the soldier said. "But I have my orders." Wheeling his horse around, he rode down the cliff to rejoin the rest of his squad.

Suddenly the fighting and shouting were all over. Jimmy stood with his father and Mr. Morris on the bluff and watched what was left of Camp Marks burn to the ground. Flames lit the sky for miles around. Jimmy could see the silhouettes of the Capitol and the Washington Monument, starkly black against the orange sky.

Numb with shock and exhaustion, people began

walking, heading for the Maryland woods. Mr. Morris trudged behind a straggling group.

Jimmy's father put his hand on Jimmy's shoulder. "Time to go, son. We've been away from your ma long enough."

"What about Mr. Morris? He doesn't have anyplace to go."

"What do you think we should do?" his father asked.

Jimmy didn't need to think long. "Let him come live with us. He can stay in the barn."

Mr. Watkins smiled, making smoky crinkles around his mouth. "I think that's a fine idea. But let's see if Mr. Morris wants to come with us, first."

Jimmy ran to catch up with Mr. Morris. "Me and my pa would like you to come live with us. Just for a while. Till you get to be a chef again. We have a room over the barn you can use. Will you come, please?"

Mr. Morris looked from Jimmy to his father and back to Jimmy again. When he spoke, his voice was rough with emotion. "I'd be honored to come stay with you folks. Do you think your mother would mind if I did a little cooking now and then? I like to keep my hand in."

"My wife would truly appreciate a night away from the stove," Mr. Watkins said. "Looks like we've got a long haul ahead of us. Who's game?"

"I am," Jimmy said.

"So am I," Mr. Morris replied, "though I may not look it. I might be getting on in years, but I can still hike a fair piece."

"The troops have blocked the roads," Mr. Watkins said. "So we can't go back the way we came. We'll have to hike around the long way, I'm afraid. Maybe somebody will give us a lift."

Someone did give them a lift, as far as the C.O. Canal. Then they walked along the towpath. Jimmy was too tired to watch the barges gliding down the moonlit canal. He stumbled, half asleep, and his father caught him.

Finally they reached Chain Bridge. On unsteady legs, Jimmy staggered across the bridge suspended high above the Potomac River. The three of them walked for hours, it seemed, down winding Chain Bridge Road before another car offered them a ride. Jimmy slept in the backseat, leaning against his father's shoulder, as the car rumbled down the star-washed road.

Dawn was lightening the sky with gray streaks when the driver of the car let them out and then turned down another road. "Still have a few miles," Mr. Watkins said as they set off down the highway.

Jimmy had never been out when the day was so new. Even the mockingbirds, the first birds to break the night's silence, weren't up yet.

"I don't know about you two, but my stomach's as empty as a rain barrel during the dry season," Mr. Morris said.

"We don't have any food," Jimmy's father pointed out.

"Look, Pa," Jimmy said. "Here's a whole field of corn. Ripe, too."

He climbed over the wire fence and disappeared into the tall, tasseled rows of corn. Minutes later, he brought back six ears of corn, which Mr. Morris speared on sticks. They roasted the corn over a small fire. Jimmy gnawed both ears right down to the cob. Nothing had ever tasted so good.

With their growling stomachs satisfied, they struck off down the road at a lively pace. They were going home.

"Without our bonus money," Jimmy's father said with a sigh.

"We sure tried, though," Jimmy said.

Every man in Camp Marks had tried his darnedest. Jimmy remembered the man buried in the box and the feisty O'Brians. They all faced hard times with bravery and good spirits.

"I wish I had a present to bring Ma," he said wistfully. His mother would understand why he gave his singing money to the O'Brian family, but he still wanted to give her something special. After all, she had run the farm mostly by herself these past three weeks.

Mr. Morris tapped the pocket where Jimmy kept his harmonica. "You have a present for your mother. Didn't you tell me she liked music better than anything?"

"She likes my singing," Jimmy said.

"Now you can sing *and* play a musical instrument. Your ma'll burst her buttons with pride," said Mr. Morris.

"That's not all she'll be proud about," Jimmy's father added. "Wait'll she hears how you stood up for Mr. Morris."

They passed the same house Jimmy had first noticed on their way to Washington, D.C. It seemed like years since that morning, but Jimmy couldn't figure why. The house looked exactly the same, with its sagging porch and rusty pot in the yard.

Then Jimmy realized the house hadn't changed, but *he* had. He felt like two boys. Part of him was Jimmy Crack Corn, the boy who loved to sing and make music. And part of him was James, the boy who was growing up.

The closer they got to their house, the faster Jimmy walked. When he caught sight of the barn roof, he started running. He never thought he'd be so glad to see that old garden.

Carl Brooks spotted him first. "Jimmy!" he cried,

running to meet his brother. "Ma, Jimmy and Pa are back!"

Rosemary flew out of the house. "Jimmy Crack Corn!" she squealed.

His mother came out on the porch, wiping her hands on her apron. "Who is this tall, young stranger?" she teased.

"It's me, Ma," Jimmy said. "James Watkins, Junior."

His mother gave him a kiss. "My, aren't we grown up. James now, is it?"

Jimmy was itching to play a tune on his harmonica. "Only sometimes," he said with a grin, and began to play.

Afterword

In the days following the burning of Camp Marks, newspapers across the country were filled with photographs of the riot. They called it "The Battle of Washington." Americans were ashamed of the way the government had treated the veterans. Most people did not vote to reelect President Hoover that November. Instead, they voted for Franklin Roosevelt, whose "New Deal" program promised to get the country back on its feet.

A second expedition of the Bonus Army marched into Washington in 1933. This time the marchers were treated quite differently. President Roosevelt sent them to Fort Hunt, where they were fed and housed decently. And he offered the veterans work in the Civilian Conservation Corps, a jobs program usually reserved for younger men.

The bonus marchers were finally rewarded. In 1936 Congress voted to give the veterans their bonus money nine years before payment was due.